This book belongs to:

_____

For Danni Corgan – J.W.

For a complete list of books by Jeanne Willis and Tony Ross visit
www.andersenpress.co.uk

This paperback edition first published in 2022 by Andersen Press Ltd.
First published in Great Britain in 2021 by Andersen Press Ltd.,
20 Vauxhall Bridge Road, London, SW1V 2SA, UK
Vijverlaan 48, 3062 HL Rotterdam, Nederland
Text copyright © Jeanne Willis, 2021.
Illustration copyright © Tony Ross, 2021.
The rights of Jeanne Willis and Tony Ross to be identified as the author
and illustrator of this work have been asserted by them in accordance
with the Copyright, Designs and Patents Act, 1988.
Printed and bound in China.
1   3   5   7   9   10   8   6   4   2
British Library Cataloguing in Publication Data available.
ISBN 978 1 78344 953 8

OLD MACDONALD had a PHONE

JEANNE WILLIS

TONY ROSS

ANDERSEN PRESS

♫ ♪ Old Macdonald had a phone ♫ ♪

And it was very smart,

It helped him organise his farm

And fill his shopping cart...

♪ Old Macdonald had a phone
He dropped it in the lake.

He ordered one online but...

Bought a hundred by mistake!

They were taken by the cows,
The boars and the sows,
The rooster, sheep and hens
And all their furry friends.

♪ ♪ Everybody had a phone ♪♪
And it was such good fun!

Nobody would put them down
So nothing else got done.

♫ The rooster didn't crow, ♪

The horse wouldn't go...

The sheep ignored the rams,
The sheepdog lost the lambs.

Old Macdonald had a farm
But nothing in his shop,

Cows messaging at milking time
Would not produce a drop.

♪ The hens wouldn't lay, 🎵
On their phones all day,

Here a tweet, there a chat,
WhatsApping the farm cat.

♪ Old Macdonald used to run ♪
The noisiest of farms,
Now all he hears are ring tones
And the beep of phone alarms.

Old Macdonald took the phones
And locked them in the shed,
It made the sheepdog so annoyed,
He sulked and went to bed.

The fox scared the sheep,

The rooster stayed asleep,

The bull refused to sweep
His manure in a heap...

Young Macdonald found his dad
Sobbing in his van,
"Smart phones aren't
so bad," he said.
"Get with the times, old man."

"Like all technology,
If we use it sensibly
And live life to the full,
Then phones are cool."

They had a meeting at the farm
With all the animals,
And promised to give back the phones
If they obeyed these rules:
A chat-chat here, and a selfie there,
But not all day! Does that sound fair?

♪ The creatures at Macdonald's Farm ♫
Agreed with what was said.
They limited their phone time,
And they ran the farm instead.

♪ The eggs were laid, ♪

The milk was made...

They all had a party
Now the bills were paid!

♪ ♪ All the creatures on the farm ♫♫
Are happy as can be,
They talk to one another
And they do not text at tea.

♫ Rooster crows at dawn, ♪
The sheep are shorn...

Lots of little pigs

And lambs are born...

♫ Best of all, Macdonald's bull ♪
Won first prize in the show,

And everybody texted...

Smiley Face, YOLO! YOLO!

Read more in this online-safety series by Jeanne Willis and Tony Ross:

STAYING SAFE

ONLINE BULLYING

SOCIAL MEDIA

For more information and teaching resources,
visit www.andersenpress.co.uk/online-safety